BALANCE -

THE NEW RELIGION

A chance to mine the diamond within you…

Aayushi Mehta

Chennai • Bangalore

CLEVER FOX PUBLISHING
Chennai, India

Published by CLEVER FOX PUBLISHING 2022

ISBN: 978-93-94437-36-4

CONTENTS

PREFACE

This book first came into being when I sat down to start journaling, after months of being at home. It was a rainy night. As I journaled my thoughts, I decided to do it with meaning - as if I was explaining the events of my life to an audience. After day one of journaling, I understood how therapeutic it was and continued doing it every day. As I wrote more, I identified one common trait in all the experiences I wrote each day—it lacked *balance*. I, thus, decided to base each written topic on *balance*. Soon, I made my family members read my version of a memoir and they were in awe. They encouraged me to write more and eventually it materialised into a whole book. Throughout my journey in becoming one with my mental illnesses and recovering from it, I searched for an idol - someone who shared their journey and managed to get out of it successfully. I searched for someone like me. There was no one who shared the terrifying details - someone who I could empathise with. For some reason the subject was still a taboo and many are scared to share the truth. With this in mind, I promised myself that if I could get out of the turmoil and recover completely, I would share my story to help those who need guidance and hope; to show them that if an ordinary teenager like me can crawl out of the illness, so can they. Through personal experiences and incidents, I aim to showcase how exactly I was able to heal and what decisions led me to having a healthier and more positive outlook to life.

The book is created in such a way that one can read any chapter at any time without having to read the previous chapter. The book is like a guardian angel by your bedside. Anytime you feel like you are losing your mental balance and need help, you can read a chapter - whichever feels the most appropriate for the time.

PART I

DAY 1/30

A sob story is what some may connote from the events that lead to the uncoverings of this new religion. A religion where you are your own inner God and where the world is before you to mould. A religion where heaven and hell are the two places made by you. A religion where ultimate peace and tranquillity are only unlocked by the key of balance. How is this balance achieved? The simple answer is - experience. An experience shaped by your hands.

It was a cold, autumn morning. It was not only the first day of school, but the first day of senior school. The feelings of terror combined with the excitement of wearing non-uniform to school. The difference in hierarchy. The professional treatment by teachers. All the little aspects that changed school experience from grade eight to nine. Change - my biggest fear. A pair of brand-new, blue jeans and a yellow jumper was my attire for day one. The night before, I created a minor earthquake across the whole house to make sure I packed everything. Unfortunately, I got stuck in English class. I forgot my binder. The biggest equipment I had to pack. Disappointing others - another fright of mine. When I was confronted about this in front of the whole class, instead of confidently speaking the truth and owning up to a simple mistake, I felt the rush of tears swelling up in my eyes. Down they dropped one by one like a slight drizzle, which eventually turned into a small storm. Confused. My teacher and classmates were all confused as to why I started weeping. Facing my fears was what it actually was. Judgement from friends and the teacher was all that resulted. Overthinking was step two. I pondered about this incident the whole day. It chewed me up. My attention span in classes that day slightly wavered and class participation was miniscule.

"How was your first day back at school?"

I detested it. Unsurprisingly, I had a large pile of homework. It took me double the time as for the perfectionist I was. Making mistakes - another fear.

This was the first time my fears of change, disappointing others and making mistakes came out for the world to see and were recognisable. It was the first time I felt vulnerable. However, it was also the first time I felt balanced. Every yin quality has a yang counterpart.

Thought of the day: Vulnerability does not show weakness, it shows strength.

DAY 2/30

Yin and Yang is a Chinese philosophical concept that showcases how opposite and contrary forces may actually be complementary, interdependent and interconnected in the natural world, and how they may arise from each other as they interrelate to one another. Yin and Yang were known to be separate entities of the human being. An anecdotal reference to this clearly depicts the idea.

It was in August 2019 that I joined a new school. With my three fears intact, the complexities of anxiety started emerging. Again, the first day of school was a disaster. I had almost forgotten to take my bags from the taxi and thought I embarrassed myself. I came home sobbing and shivering. I started overthinking the entire day and how some people did not even bother getting to know me. That very day, my mother, baffled and perplexed, took me to meet one of my school friends. This friend saw me unstable and was in a state of awe. School was made a whole lot better from that day onwards as she had one of my shoulders. The other shoulder was backed up by her soulmate. Soulmates - people who are destined to be in each other's paths so they both can give each other love and encouragement when needed, to keep going on their earthly odyssey. Like this, they both had my back. We were unstoppable and unbreakable - like the three musketeers. In the two years of my time at this school, we saw each other's highs and lows lower than low. The question that now stems is: What exactly was the superglue to this friendship? The simple answer is Yin and Yang. The Yin and Yang energy worked like a magnetic form of balance. Energy switching was also involved. The negative qualities of one person would be cancelled out by the positive qualities of the other. The Yin of one person attracted the Yang of the other subconsciously. Obviously, it was the Yang and Yang that got along. The two soulmates worked in this way. Then, there was me, being held by a Yin on one shoulder and a Yang on the other; where both humans changed their roles on a constant basis to maintain the balance. The friendship worked a bit like a weighing scale, where I was the pointer in between and the soulmates were constantly adjusting their scale pans to keep the ultimate balance and sustain the friendship.

Just like Yin and Yang is present within us, it has an equal effect on our outside world and the relationships we foster.

Thought of the day: Strong friendships require outlashes of negative qualities as much as it does positive ones.

DAY 3/30

Jainism is an ancient Indian religion that teaches a path to spiritual purity and enlightenment through disciplined non-violence. The three main pillars of Jainism are ahiṃsā (non-violence), anekāntavāda (non-absolutism), and aparigraha (asceticism). While often employing concepts shared with Hinduism and Buddhism, the result of a common cultural and linguistic background, the Jain tradition is regarded as an independent phenomenon rather than as a Hindu sect or a Buddhist heresy.

Growing up, I was part of a large Jain community. However, I never quite fitted in with the norms completely. I had my boundaries with rituals, fasting, and other religious procedures. Additionally, I only took up what resonated from the religion. When the question arouses to me: What religion do you follow? My brain says Jainism, but my heart yells Balance - a bit of every religion. I believe in Christianity, Buddhism and all others. From my childhood, I have memories of going to a vast variety of cathedrals, churches, ashrams, as well as temples. One would expect me to feel differently for every place I went; the truth is that I did. Those different feelings are attached to my heart to create the balanced feeling of fulfilment. I always wondered how I would feel with only one religion to follow. A heart filled with a single emotion and a single perspective. No balance, but mere satisfaction and wholeness of one kind. I slightly struggled with this as I always assumed that I was judged for not complying with the norms. Judgement - another fear. Not knowing how to do 'pooja' (a ritual to worship and show respect to God), moreover, entering temples of other religions were some of the reasons I got frowned upon by some. I always questioned my parents as to why we were not like the others. Today, nonetheless, I am grateful for it. Despite feeling like an outsider even when being inside, the fact that my parents nurtured me in an open-minded manner has made me a well-rounded individual. A non-judgmental, respectful girl who accepts everything with a well-balanced heart and brain. Not delving too much into a single religion has enabled me to think with my heart and my brain at the right times.

Here again, the idea of balance is lucid. Not only was it fabricated in my body with my brain and heart, but also with positive and negative qualities. It worked a bit like an equation this time, where a negative starter of judgement by others was balanced with positive results of my inner qualities.

Thought of the day: Life is an equation that you devise.

DAY 4/30

"Actions speak more than words." It is a well-known proverb that many live by. Here is a short dissection of it. Actions and words are both non-tangible; however, they have very different results. Actions and words can both be positive or negative. They are also in some sense counterparts. Words lead to actions, or vice versa.

It was during ninth grade that I experienced the biggest blow with high-school drama. Ironically, my high-school drama led to an unsuccessful Shakespearean drama show. A week before the show, one of my best friends had told me about two of our friends dating. Afraid of the community's pressures and judgements, they understandably left it confidential. When I met another of my best friends, I told her. It was wrong, but wouldn't anyone tell their number one? But I didn't stop there. I got some sort of satisfaction by spreading the word in a secretive and positive manner to help the couple. I thought telling another close friend would do no harm. I thought that if people of our age knew, it would only make their life easier. I cared too much. Their business had wrongfully become mine. I made decisions for them. As expected, though, it hit me in the face hard. The second friend I had confided in spread the word and claimed it was a rumour. It's funny what they say about karma. This felt like a wrecking ball in my gut. I knew I was wrong, even if my intentions were never harmful. I immediately apologised to all the parties involved.

Sadly, it did not end there. A group of boys in my year decided to use this to make fun of me. This was worse. I felt worthless - a joke. It was the night before I had to present *Macbeth*. The group of boys called me. They laughed and enjoyed me crying on the phone - instead of articulating the lines of the play, I puked out tears that night. I was the main character in the play. My class was counting on me. When the day finally came, I remember trying to memorise the lines in the car. I did not have butterflies in my stomach, instead, I had wasps - an entire beehive. We had to run the show twice. The first time, I froze and started shivering. My anxiety kicked in. This was very unlike me, hence, my teacher pulled me aside. When she heard my situation, she calmly said, "Then do this for them. Show them what you are actually made of. You are a fighter." The second round was more successful than the first. The room kept crowding up as the lines magically came out of my mouth.

Every word and action will have a balanced consequence. Sometimes, when unbalanced and unfair, events eventually play into place to become equal.

Thought of the day: Keeping your nose out of unnecessary business makes relationships easier.

DAY 5/30

Parents are known to be the two pillars in one's life. Imagine being the ceiling and your parents being the pillars holding it up. A family is like an architectural complex, where support is key. Each aspect counts on the other. Every part has got the other's support.

It was the summer of grade eight and end-of-year exams were coming up. Stress was a lingering emotion in my brain. My brain was the hanger and stress was the clothing hung on it. These exams were vital - they tested everything I learnt during the entire year. Preparations were rigorous, too rigorous, in fact. In school, I was a bit of a nerd. I had no trust in myself. I let stress lead the way rather than trust. I would study each chapter twice and spend the entire day studying. I would decide not to go out with friends and family. I had made myself believe that I enjoyed the process of revision. But subconsciously, I wanted the amusement. I had the longing desire to go out and enjoy myself. However, I created a jail in my room for myself. I made myself believe it was paradise. During my school days, I often prioritised work over my family and friends. It was around the end-of-year exams that my mother had an operation on her leg. It was either going to support and help her, or it was continuing with revision. My gut told me to study, but my heart scolded me to go. I argued with my family members and stayed home to revise. It was the most haunting revision session I had had. Every line I memorised morphed into words that related to hospitals, operations and injuries. As I flipped through the pages of the books, I heard voices. This was the first time I experienced voices in my head. The voices were like alarm bells ringing to make sure I went to my mother. I heard my mother's screams echoing. Still, I sat still. It wasn't too late to go, but I decided to sit untouched and study. Immense guilt is what I felt when everyone returned from the hospital. The architectural structure had collapsed - its ceiling had come crashing down. I messed up the balance. I had shown no empathy or support to my own mother. I had cared too much about what my friends and teachers would think about the grades I would receive in my exams. My priorities lied outside the house.

Just like parents maintain balance by supporting the children, the children also ought to support the parents.

Thought of the day: When the gut confuses, listen to your heart.

DAY 6/30

Best friend - an overused term used by many. It is defined as one's closest friend. Someone who understands you like no other. Someone who is there for you through thick and thin. Someone who understands your negative and less compelling side.

A best friend will help you clean up your messes no matter how disgusting you made the situation.

Growing up I had more than one best friend. In ninth grade it was one. She is one of the reasons for my current existence. It was in seventh grade when we tied the knot and promised to never leave each other's sides. Everything was blue skies and yellow sunflowers, until ninth grade. In ninth grade my best friend had experienced a tough time. She was bullied. Bullied is an understatement. The entire class made fun of her. She was left out during projects, recess and lunch. She was made fun of for her appearance, gait and anything else she did. The class made it difficult for her to simply breathe. The rest is her story to tell. I, however, experienced a sort of peer pressure. I was afraid I would undergo the same treatment, hence I decided to go rogue. I morphed into a barbie, I was fake. Instead of standing up for her, I joined in on the bullying. This slowly broke me on the inside. I would come home crying and not knowing why. I was terrified of school and the person I had become there. Teachers would come and talk to me to try to help her out. All I would say is, "I am trying."

"Try harder," is what they would reply. Slowly, as she broke and closed the doors to her heart, so did I. I became quiet, shy and would never speak to new people at gatherings. I had guilt filled up in my stomach and sadness in my heart. I could not hold this for long enough though. I vomited this guilt over the summer of that year. I apologised for everything and explained to her my side of the story. She was a warrior in this situation. She not only got through the year but was ready to give our friendship another try. This was one of the happiest days of my life. Slowly we worked on our friendship and my stomach slowly emptied itself of the guilt. My heart, on the other hand, was blemished with memories. The sadness still remains. However, her presence in my life balances the pain.

The mere presence of people in your life can have the ability to balance the negative memories or feelings associated with them.

Thought of the day: Presence helps heal, but ego results in the opposite.

DAY 7/30

Hard work always pays off, is the motto many live by. What exactly is hard work? It is when one puts in a great deal of effort and endurance. It is when the end goal is what one works their utmost best towards - the rest is blurred.

During my years in the ninth and tenth grades, I was a hard worker. I worked too hard. I studied about six hours every day after school. Additionally, I worked almost the entire day on weekends. Even if I went out, I would be restless. I would have a dictionary of "what ifs" in my head. Failing was all I contemplated. Failure - another fear of mine. I had chained myself to my room. My room had become my prison that I chose to be locked in. I would take triple the amount of time for all my tasks and then only would I reward myself with lunch, snacks or breakfast. This was how the years passed. During my final IGCSE exams this mindset was at its peak. The first exam was mathematics. I had spent weeks preparing; nevertheless, I still felt ill-equipped. It was my overthinking that kicked in. Thoughts of potential failure ran down the staircase along my brain. The exam, to my surprise, went very well. Next was history. It was the night before this exam that all hell broke loose. Everything I had revised felt like a tornado in my head - all there but not there at the same time. It was swerving with a large hollow space in between that made the information feel invisible and not present. The feeling was fierce. It took a toll on my confidence and anxiety flowed through my entire body. It flowed from all organs to the direction of my brain. There, it turned into sadness. I shed tears the entire evening.

"I do not want to live anymore."

I chanted the words for the first time. I scraped and scratched my arms; I strangled myself with a scarf; I tried jumping out the balcony. I even started writing a suicide letter. It was only a couple hours before my final exam and I was a thought away from suicide. This was when my father came into the room.

"Why don't you take a short nap? I will wake you up tomorrow. Tomorrow is for you to shape however you want," he said.

It was a trap. I fell asleep as he had planned, but I woke up at three o'clock. The night before had become obscure to me - a blur. I was filled with dopamine. I decided to complete some last-minute revision for four hours in the morning and was confident for an exam for the first time ever. When I finished the exam, I was more satisfied than ever. I felt accomplished. I felt balanced.

What I studied for those four hours led me to feel more balanced than what I studied in weeks. Quality speaks more than quantity.

Thought of the day: Only donkeys work hard. Work smart.

DAY 8/30

Psychotherapy is only for psychos or abnormal people. This is misunderstood by people regarding psychotherapy. As a matter of fact, psychotherapy is needed by everyone to some extent. Psychotherapy is the utilisation of psychological methods, based on regular personal interaction, in order to aid a person in changing behaviour, increasing happiness and overcoming problems.

It was in the beginning of eleventh grade, when I moved schools, that I started therapy. It was when change in my life was at its peak. Change, as mentioned before, is one of my biggest fears. I had no coping mechanisms and was in desperate need of a toolbox for rewiring. I was ashamed and conscience-stricken at first. I felt like I was missing half of my body - deranged and demented. Nevertheless, I needed this therapy. Everyday, I would be terrified to enter the taxi in the mornings. The early grey mornings with fog above the heads was a clear representation of my feelings too. My heart felt covered by heavy clouds and my brain froze in the cold. The entire taxi ride in the morning would have me overthinking. My brain would tremble to think of how I would greet my new friends when I entered the school. I would listen to music; however, the lyrics of every song would be modified and overpowered by the voices in my head. This excessive overthinking was why I went every Wednesday to therapy. It was day one of therapy. Stress was running a marathon through my body as I waited to meet my therapist. Finally, she entered - a young, sweet and composed lady.

I was petrified for the session. I had never shared my deepest and darkest secrets with anyone. The session started and the words came out like they were falling down a slide to form the events of my life in utter detail. From then on, psychotherapy sessions started to become my highlight of the week. I had a place to let out my emotions. Therapy was a well which got filled with the rain of tears from my sadness.

One session stood out from the others. In order to enable me to deal with the voices in my head, my therapist told me to sit on a chair and I had to imagine I was sitting on the empty chair placed in front of me. I had to talk to myself as though I was all the voices that tore me down. I said all the barbarous and harsh thoughts to myself and went through the emotions with my therapist. This felt like meditation - the complete opposite in actions, but the same in result.

After every session of therapy, where I usually discussed events and emotions, I was finally able to feel both sides of my body. The imbalanced feeling withered away. Sensations started to come back to the numb side of my body.

Thought of the day: Everyone has a numb part of their body and therapy is the anti-numbing ointment.

DAY 9/30

Metabolism - the scientific term for the chemical processes that take place in one's body, in order to maintain life. Having a fast metabolism means that one's metabolic processes consistently burn up more calories in a given time compared to an average person.

Growing up I have always had a quick metabolism. The reactions of my organs, including my brain, were always rapid. This resulted in me being underweight and lanky for majority of my life. "Skinny", "malnourished" and "anorexic" were only a fraction of the words that my mother and I had to hear from people. "It is not in our control" would be our go-to phrase every time. It had reached a point where it became the storyline of my life. Eventually, the way in which I looked started to define who I was. People would start making assumptions about my personality. She is weak-minded and spineless; she is inexpressive; she is frail and feeble. Gradually, without realising it, I started believing in these assumptions. My world started becoming constructed by those around me. I lost myself in the whirlpool of others' words. I felt as though I was drowning. I had no idea the person I was anymore.

"Who am I?" The question was taped across my forehead. Every time I would look into the mirror, I would see an insecure, young and lonely girl with melancholy hiding behind the pupils of her empty gaze. I longed for someone's hand to pull me out of the constant spinning of negative thoughts. This is where tennis and dance came into play in my life. They were the two hands that pulled me out of the spinning desolation. I started practising tennis from a young age. I played for about eight years. Playing on the court every week made me feel powerful. My use of mind-tactics, as well as being a speedy player, woke up the emotions of strength and power in my brain. It had felt as though those feelings were in hibernation all my life. The sweat felt like a trophy I had achieved and it made me feel like I had come to one with myself. My appearance had no impact and control over what I was capable of achieving. With dance, the emotion of confidence grew like a protective shield around my body. Performing the dance steps with utter grace and finesse allowed me to start loving the body my spirit is in. I danced for eight years. Practising both sports in the last two years let the emotions of power and confidence form a blanket I would comfort myself in.

It was only when I started to find joy in tennis and dance that they were able to influence the vestibular system and maintain balance in my life - balance that allowed me to look in the mirror and see the person I truly was.

Thought of the day: Mirrors show the reflection of what we feel, not how we look.

DAY 10/30

An overbite is a malocclusion - a deviation or misalignment from the regular alignment of teeth. Overbites happen when the upper teeth stick out too far beyond the lower teeth.

As a baby and toddler, I always had trouble sleeping. I would start crying when the sun was in the west and continue until it rose in the east. This is because I had severe nightmares - another one of my fears. Strangely, the dreams from my childhood are still vivid. A few, particularly, still stand out. In the first one, I remember being present at a construction site. I was on the top floor of the building being built. There, bombings started and I was stuck. People with guns were present and they began shooting. There was outright destruction everywhere around me. Helplessness, not fear, was what I felt As I was a young impotent child. In the second one, I was at home. There was a fire around my house. People were screaming and yelling for help. Again, instead of feeling alarmed and fearful, I was a helpless toddler. Helplessness - another one of my fears.

One night, however, after a vast time span, I slept the entirety of the night. There was something different though

- I had my thumb in my mouth. Having my thumb in my mouth, for some reason, made me feel stronger and in control. This habit lasted for ten years. It was for ten years that I needed my thumb in my mouth at night to avoid feeling unbalanced, endangered and incapable. The thumb-taking caused me to have an overbite. This was a symbol of weakness and vulnerability. A symbol of darkness. Growing up with this, I was name-called for it quite often. I was compared to animals and made to feel what is perceived to be "unattractive". It was not long before I almost broke into pieces of diffidence that my dentist told me I needed braces. I had the idiosyncrasy of feeling excited, as people are usually scared of the process. It was finally my turn and the orthodontist stuck each metal piece one by one. Each piece was reminiscent of a soldier fighting the feelings that led to nightmares every night. Finally, he was done. I had underestimated the pain. The soldiers were defending me, but had to push backwards to defend me in the most optimum manner. Years of changing the bands was what kept the braces intact. Years of having soldiers to defend me. Years of practising to eventually fight the bad dreams mentally.

It took four years to learn how to balance my brain with emotions that make me feel perseverant and resilient, to eventually fight the frightening dreams without having my thumb in my mouth.

Thought of the day: Bad habits are band-aids that conceal some of our greatest fears.

DAY 11/30

Dark circles are naturally present to some people. The skin under the eyes is thinner than the rest of the skin. Dark circles are heredity - an inherited physical trait from birth. It can also be caused by the dilation of blood vessels under your eyes.

"Do you sleep enough?" is a question I got a lot of growing up. The opposite is what I experienced. As a baby, I would not sleep so much; however, as I grew up, I overslept. I slept for about seven to nine hours every night. If I had not received that sleep at night, I would sleep in the afternoon or evening. When I would tell people I slept so much, their sudden jaw drop would instantly cause me to chuckle. Why was it that I slept so much? The answer lies in emptiness. As a teenager, I always felt as though I was a walking kettle. Most days, if people did not fill me up with the water of warm words, I felt hollow. My happiness relied on others; the judgement and opinion of others. Sleeping was a getaway for me - an escape. I felt as though I would fill the empty kettle with my own thoughts - water that was just the right temperature and amount. I could fill it with potential scenarios. In comparison to having no control over my thoughts when I slept as a baby and toddler, the situations developed into having complete control. This control over thoughts was at its peak when I had crushes on people. Everyone has those few people they crushed on in high school. I, too, had my fair share. It was the texting phase that I loved. I fished for compliments from people at the time. The compliments turned the warm water in the kettle into masala chai. It added extra flavour, making sleep even more unwinding and peaceful. It was in twelfth grade that I experienced this in its finest form. I had a crush on someone and I gradually began to like that person. I had experienced small crushes, yes, but I had never experienced fully liking someone. This person made sleeping every night much more tranquil. This person made me feel like a kettle filled with masala chai every day. When I realised that it would not work out, I knew I slowly had to accept it. Suddenly, the masala chai turned into burned coffee. I blamed myself for it. I made myself feel less. Sleepless nights were the consequence. I reached a point where the coffee became so burnt that I knew I had to empty it.

I realised that I needed a filter, to reboot and start over, to balance my life. I needed a life with quality sleep where I could control my thoughts - the masala and the sugar, preventing the formation of burnt coffee. I needed sleep where I could also revamp my thoughts - empty the chai and remake it to taste as good as the previous lot.

Thought of the day: See the twinkle in the eyes, not the dark circles.

DAY 12/30

Travelling is a hobby that many enjoy. For some, it is for recreation, while for others it is simply because their work makes it obligatory.

Growing up, I have travelled to multiple places around the globe. We, as a family, would take trips to India twice a year and travel to places in Europe during the spring and Easter breaks. My favourite trips were those where we got the chance to discover the attractive cities in India other than Mumbai. It was our trip to Jaipur that stood out to me the most. There was something about the forts there that made me feel protected and regal. From the first day of the visit itself, the majestic creations made me feel as though I had blue blood running through my vessels. The staff had poured rose petals on my head as I entered the palace-like hotel. Every fort I entered, I felt the aroma of grandeur. The stories associated with each of the attractions were even more glorious. Jaipur's Nahargarh Fort is enticing even though it is not as massive and eye-catching as Amber and Jaigarh. Nahargarh Fort is set on the Aravallis and offers some alluring views of the Pink City. Along with Amber and Jaigarh, Nahargarh once served as the defence ring for

Jaipur. It was built in 1734 by Sawai Jai Singh, the then king of Jaipur, mainly as a retreat for the queens and the king. While much of its glory is lost with changing times, the fort still stands strong under the Rajasthan sun. Stories about why the king built the fort and what each fort comprised, in terms of the way they were built, was very intriguing. The experience of walking in and out of the forts, taking in the views, was what I looked forward to every time. On the other hand, there were our family trips to the USA and the European countries. Here, too, we were fortunate to experience monuments and attractions. However, they were different and almost opposite to those in India. Their histories were more political. The museums, bridges and monumental structures had their own unique stories. Other attractions were the theme parks. The fun derived from these places was due to adrenaline rushes, rather than appreciation for aesthetics. This, nonetheless, did not make the fun any less, enabling me to feel balanced.

My trips around the world worked like a compass. If we travelled to a place emblematic of the north one year, we would travel to a place representative of the south the other year. Same with east and west. This maintained a balanced intake of information about the countries, allowing us to become well-rounded people.

Thought of the day: Life is a compass in the hand that allows one to lead the direction.

DAY 13/30

Identity - the set of qualities and beliefs that make one person or group different from others. What defines an identity and its relative characteristics? The answer lies in one's personal experiences and what is concluded from those experiences.

As a teenager, I always had identity issues. I had a lack of identity. I tried to be what others wanted me to be. This was where the fear of judgement rooted from. This lack of identity also originated from the fact that small changes or stressors in life were made to seem bigger from my perspective. This identity crisis caused me to have early stages of mood swings in my teenage years. Every time these mood swings would come knocking on the door of my brain, it would send signals for either releasing happy hormones or depressed hormones. I had not experienced the extremes of the happy hormones yet; whereas I experienced multiple instances of contemplating to put a full stop to my story. Only one person knew about these - my younger brother. The first attempt was, as mentioned before, around the time of one of my IGCSE exams. It was my overthinking and lack of identity that often led to the outbursts. The outbursts were primarily caused by the pain of others - when others would tell me their problems or difficulties, my heart would get bruised. It was like their pain was transmitted to my body through the valves of my heart - eventually getting pumped to the rest of the body. It was extremely hard for me to help others as I was struggling with finding my inner self. I was struggling with what my true purpose was. Every time I attempted to do so, I ended up hurting people. I would have to apologise immediately to form band-aids on my heart. Another reason for my outbursts was the negative opinions or harsh words from others. This would make my heart seem like a punching bag, as I would say nothing to stand up for myself. The only way to stop the punching, from my perspective, was shutting down. There is a graphic memory of me magically finding myself on the balcony. It was as though I was teleported. One second, I was in my room in a pool of tears and the next, I was leaning outwards in the cold air.

That night, I could not control my feelings. My feelings were like the traffic lights. It was red. Orange. Almost green and suddenly I felt hands embracing my entire body, balancing my body, so it would not fall.

Pulling me away, it was my younger brother. A two-page letter was in his hands. We let it out and watched it fly away like a lantern as my body and mind slowly gained balance.

Thought of the day: Life is too precious to be burnt into the flames of one second of impetuosity.

DAY 14/30

The Golden Temple, located in Amritsar, Punjab, is not only a gurdwara (a central religious place of the Sikhs) but also a symbol of human brotherhood and equality.

One of the most impactful trips I had was to this temple. It was in the summer of 2019 that my family and I had the opportunity to visit it. As we entered, our eyes were bestowed with an awe-inspiring golden structure located on a small man-made pool. It glistened under the sun and reflected in the pellucid waters that surrounded it.

Rama and Sita are believed to have spent their fourteen-year exile in Amritsar, the epicentre of Sikhism. This shows how holy the place is. To the south of the temple was a garden and the tower of Baba Atal. The 'Guru Ka Langar' offered free food to around 20,000 people every day. The number would reach up to 100,000 on special occasions. This communal canteen was at the eastern entrance of the temple complex, and it provided free food to all visitors, regardless of colour, creed, caste or gender. Visitors to the Golden Temple had to remove their shoes and cover their heads before entering the temple. Even without shoes, there was not a speck of dust that stuck to the feet. This was because of how the worshipers, no matter where they were from, cleaned the marble together every night to make it incandescent under the sun every morning. The Granth Sahib was kept in the Temple during the day and kept in the Akal Takht or Eternal Throne in the night. The Akal Takht also housed the ancient weapons used by the Sikh warriors. The rugged old Jubi Tree in the north-west corner of the compound is believed to possess special powers. It was planted 450 years ago, by the Golden Temple's first high priest, Baba Buddha. The temple was built at a level lower than the surrounding land level. The holy shrine has four entrances on all four directions signifying that people belonging to every walk of life are equally welcome. The trip to this temple taught me the lesson of egalitarianism, humility and selflessness. All these three qualities formed the most important ingredients needed to follow the religion of balance. Not only The way the structures were created but the reasons behind it also provided a sense of balance. After this trip, I had a eureka moment.

What if the ideologies imposed during the creation of the Golden Temple were applied by everyone in their respective lives? What if the creation of the religion of balance relied merely on taking in ingredients, i.e., significant qualities, from various religions like Sikhism? Balance is like a bowl of salad with vegetables or ingredients from every religion.

Thought of the day: Follow the religion that you create.

DAY 15/30

Grandparents - those who fill in the gaps left by our parents. Technically, every human has two sets of grandparents - two that are maternal and two that are paternal. For some, every grandparent is alive, whereas, for others only a few still walk the Earth.

Growing up, I have always been my nani's (maternal grandmother) pet. I always looked up to her. An independent woman that runs her own business - a rarity in her generation. I would always go to her jewellery boutique and learn from her. She never belittled my naive brain and took me seriously even if I was underaged. She allowed me to design jewellery for her and even created and sold two pieces. The experience aided my skills immensely. In addition to this, I loved spending time with her. We would often go on lunch or coffee dates and discover the new hotspots in Mumbai. Also, we loved playing board games together. Sequence, Phase 10, Monopoly Deal, Card games, name a board game and we have probably tried it. Nana, my maternal grandfather, and I would enjoy going through collations together. We loved going through his stamp collections; looking through memory books; moreover, reading through his writings about his trips around the globe. At night, the three of us would enjoy storytelling, either about my nani's dog - the infamous Poppy Doggy, or about my nana's naughty childhood. For my father's side, I barely got time to spend with my dada, my paternal grandfather, as he passed away when I was quite young. My dadi, paternal grandmother, on the other hand, spent a lot of time with me. We would have daily gossip sessions about the Bollywood world; discuss meal recipes; furthermore, go on multiple shopping sprees. She was the finest diva, with the biggest heart. I look up to her too. I highly appreciated her optimistic mentality despite living alone. Unfortunately, I understood my grandparents' value in my life only when I was deprived of their presence. Their simple existence influenced me to become the most modest and mature version of myself. With them and their wisdom, I was treated like someone way beyond my years. What I lacked at home with my immediate family, I attained with my grandparents.

Life at home was like a weighing scale. Sometimes it got out of balance. My grandparents were like the extra materials on both sides that enabled life to retrieve balance and have purpose. Their wisdom and experience were vital for the balance in life. Relations with sagacious people allows life to regain its equilibrium.

Thought of the day: Age is just a costume.

DAY 16/30

Art - the expression or application of human creative skill and imagination, typically in a visual form, producing works to be appreciated primarily for their beauty or emotional power.

I have always had a knack for art and eye for creativity. I enjoyed it as it was a form of processing my thoughts and feelings. It was a coping mechanism. When I was younger, I went to art classes held by the government. The tasks that were given at the class were ambiguous. I thoroughly liked this as towards the end of the lesson, I was able to determine my emotions and truly become one with my moods. Art helped with my emotions. Every time I felt as though I was tipping towards an extreme side, I would pick out a pencil and paper and start sketching. My expressive side would come raging out like a racing car, impulsively and unusually fast. My hands were the racing car and the paper was the track. At a young age, I never understood my talent. I always thought it was normal to work in bursts. My teachers would always say, “Your works depict a very expressive artist.”

I never took it seriously at the time as all my artworks looked the same to me. They all had the same finishing. Art was therapy for me when I was in eleventh grade. At that age, I started going to private classes. I had to create artworks for school, but at the same time the creations helped me cope with my extreme feelings. In eleventh grade, I was struggling to find myself. I had multiple, depressive episodes and often underwent the extremes of feeling low. Saturdays became a garbage truck, where I dumped all the negative emotions of the week in huge chunks. Every time I would show my artworks to my parents, they would start off with a face of great admiration, but then look at each other with a perturbed glance. This always confused me. Little did I know that beneath the layers of the lines, shapes and forms was a disturbed and lonely girl. Beneath the layers was a girl that could not control her feelings, making her feel isolated in a world surrounded by people. Beneath the layers was a girl trying to discover her true potential, yelling to be freed and taken out of the metaphorical prison made by her inner demons.

The expression of my feelings onto paper allowed the extremes of my emotions to finally meet, resulting in me feeling more collected and balanced.

Thought of the day: Some of the most creative answers lie within you.

DAY 17/30

Music can be defined as the vocal or instrumental sounds combined in a manner to produce beauty of form, harmony and expression of emotion.

Growing up, I have always been passionate about music. Listening to music, the differing and unique beats, would cause different emotions in my body to emerge. Music had the soothing effect of calming bells in temples or windchimes. I would listen to music of genres that arouse opposing emotions to what I felt at the time. In car rides, I would often overthink. My thoughts unwound like a never-ending scroll. When I looked out the window, the trees slowly morphed into the characters of my thoughts. Sometimes, it was haunting as all I wanted to do was enjoy the scenic views and relax. Hence, every time I set foot into the car, we turned the music on. It soothed my thoughts and made it more positive. The music allowed me to feel my toes and stay present in the physical world. The same happened to me in the shower. I always took almost an hour to shower. The warm water covering my body was like a switch on my brain that turned on the thoughts. Every sprinkle of water that touched my body sent an electrical signal to and from cells, glands and muscles all over my body. This would also cause me to struggle with finding the right balance within my brain and my motor, sensory and autonomic structures within my eyes. While in the shower, the plain white wall in front of me turned into a hollow tunnel. A hollow space filled with rows of the thoughts of my imagination. There was no light at the end of the tunnel. It was a simple void filled with forms of my thoughts. In my parents' view, I was just wasting the warm water and having a ball in it. What actually took place was me getting sucked into an illusion of pure darkness. My parents would often knock on the door to make sure I did not fall asleep. The characters of my imagination were often frightening. Phantasm was what it was more like. I would thus close my eyes to avoid the spine-chilling feelings. The same would happen when I would look into the mirror. The mirror, which was fogged up by the heat of the water, would slowly turn into layers of the stories created by my mind. I would often stare into it to uncover the ideas that layered up to form the thoughts in my head. The emptiness that I felt caused me to overthink about every little event that took place in my life and every possible event that could take place. This would cause me to remain gazing into the foggy and coated mirror. This was why I listened to music when I showered. It made me see the white wall and the covered mirror before me in their true forms.

It prevented me from leaving the external reality. It allowed my brain and eyes to remain balanced so that I remained present in the real world. Perhaps if I had opened up about this at an early age, I would have gained the lacking balance I longed for.

Thought of the day: Music is the vacuum cleaner and your thoughts are the dust.

DAY 18/30

A mood swing is a sudden or intense change in emotional state. During a mood swing, a person would quickly switch from feeling upbeat and happy to feeling sad, depressed and low.

Growing up with a seesaw of emotions, I slowly realised that it was my choice as to how I wanted it to affect me. Either I could let it impede certain activities or I could learn to use it to my advantage. The latter was what I attempted to do. I started doing tasks based on how I felt, rather than a logical order of when they were due. I ensured that I did not procrastinate too much but working closer to the date at times only pushed me to work harder. This made the IB more of a balanced course for me, than IGCSE where I over studied. I attained the same level of marks for the IB in comparison to IGCSE; however, I was more content and happy. Additionally, during the IB, I had learnt the art of balancing school and social life. Since I did schoolwork according to what my mood wanted to do, I had more time in hand. Thus, I was less stressed. This made me excited to turn into a social animal. The excursions with family or friends would be the goal I worked towards when I studied. This ensured that I had dopamine rushes before my outings. The outings allowed room for a revamping of my brain; a break so that I could continue studying with the correct mood. The way I worked was similar to that of enzymes. My mood was the enzyme and the task or outing was its respective substrate. Any obstacles, i.e., days of unexpected moods, that I would have to tackle on the way was ensuring the active site worked at its optimum level. The idea of applying this method enabled me to allow my mood swings to be my strength, rather than my weakness. It was all thanks to the control over my emotions that I achieved what I did during the last two years of school.

Mood swings are the seesaw and the amount of tasks or outings you have are the amount people placed on it. If placed mindfully, one has found the key to unlock the tool of balance; however, if done with negativity or in a haste, the seesaw goes completely out of control and out of balance.

Thought of the day: Your biggest weakness could be your greatest strength.

DAY 19/30

A sibling is one of two or more individuals who have common parents.

I grew up with one younger brother. We were like Tom and Jerry. I was Tom and he was Jerry. All the other cats were people who would harm my brother. Tom would constantly chase and annoy Jerry so that the other cats would not eat Jerry. Tom was, therefore, Jerry's secret protector. My brother and I would often squabble, but we would rarely physically fight. It would hurt us to see each other in tears. Additionally, we would never complain about each other. Rather, we would take the blame for each other. An incident from school remains well-defined in my memory. We were in the taxi on our way to school. As per usual, we removed our respective headsets. As he removed his and placed it on his head, we heard a sudden crack. It was the sound of his headphones breaking which were relatively expensive. Immediately, he looked me straight into the eyes. It was as though his soul was asking my soul for help. Yelling for help. As I looked back at him, I saw tears fill up in his eyes. They were about to pour out like a sudden storm, and I hugged him tightly. The embrace of my very arms prevented him from shedding tears.

"Do not worry, I have it under control. Just do not let out even one tear," I told him. It hurts me to see him cry. Every tear that he lets out feels like an arrow aimed and shot at my heart. At school, I noticed that his mood was not the usual the whole day. It was as though my brother's soul and mine were connected. It was as though both souls sat together on a big swing. If one wavered towards one direction, the other would have to do the same to remain on the swing, to maintain the feeling of balance. His sadness was, therefore, felt by my soul. I felt unhappy the entire day too. It made me worried too. I knew what I had to do. As we re-entered the house, I took the blame for my brother's mistake and told my parents that I accidentally broke the headset. I knew my brother would eventually confess to his mistake, but I had to be first and set an example to make him less fearful and nervous. I heard a few words of disappointment from my parents, before my brother said something. He admitted to his accident. I was so proud of him. I instantly squeezed him tightly in my arms. It was only in times like this we would allow each other to hug, as otherwise it loses meaning.

Being there for each other at times when we are low is how we nurture balance in each other's lives. The simple positive thoughts about each other when in need, also enables equilibrium.

Thought of the day: Those who care about you are just a thought away.

DAY 20/30

University - a high-level educational institution in which students study for degrees and where academic research is done.

During my last year at school, we had to apply to different universities. From the age of five, I knew I wanted to study fashion. Fashion was a means of self-expression that helped me find myself. I often dressed up as how I felt. A formal dress when I felt poised and positive; while track pants and a top on days I needed something comfortable and warm to protect me from my low feelings. Fashion, for me, was like a magical cape that I could use to hide my true self and cover it from the real world, as I looked for who I really was behind it. Fashion helped me immensely as I grew up and made me want to study it professionally and change my passion into a full-time career. Growing up, I had the dream of going to the University of the Arts, London (UAL). It had the world's most renowned fashion courses. Brexit, however, coincidentally took place the same year and all the rules for the EU had changed. Thus, my motivation to go to the universities in the UK was subconsciously shredded. It tore my motivation with complete aggression and a loud ripping noise. I thought to myself, "If only I was born a couple of years earlier, then I would not have the Brexit wall to hammer down."

For some reason, throughout my entire application for the UK, something did not sit right. It was as though I had an imaginary ulcer bothering my gut. Thankfully, I had also applied to the Netherlands. Although my brain wanted me to go to the UK, my heart screamed for Amsterdam Fashion Institute (AMFI). When I found out I got into AMFI, all the happy hormones were released to fill the usual hollowness of my body, like a jar filling up with water. The jar was filled with water; however, it was still tipping towards one side. It was only when I got the support from my parents that I felt like a balanced jar. If I had argued about going to the UK, there would have been a lingering feeling that made me feel like I was leaning towards one side, imbalanced.

The important decisions in life need a balanced opinion to be certain that one is making the right choice.

Thought of the day: What is taken away is replaced by destiny.

DAY 21/30

A hopeless romantic: Someone who loves the idea of being in love and someone who tends to think of love as a fairy-tale.

I have always believed in love at first sight and believed that there is someone out there for me that will appear one day to sweep me off my feet. I believed that my life was like all romantic movies, where I was the main character. As much as this ideology was like a cuddly bear that I slept with every night; it was also a blind spot to my reality. The very thought of having to wait for a 'perfect' someone required immense patience and often made me feel lonely. This was one of the reasons for the hollowness and emptiness I felt. I often felt as though I only owned half a heart. Every boy I talked to, in my view, did not see me the way I wanted him to. I cried for hours on the phone with friends to figure out why I was still single. The word "single" was like a contestant on stage and I was the judge. Every next contestant was "single" dressed up differently. There was a never ending line of "singles", hence I would never find the answer. The answer simply lies in self-love and self-confidence.

One of the most impactful and significant incidents took place on one of my senior trips. Before the senior trip, I had a bet with my friends, whether I would meet a special someone on the trip. My friends betted for yes, while I opted for no. It was the first night of the trip. We all freshened up to look our best. We entered the dance club. The club was filled with Dutch people; thus, obviously they brought their flare and tendencies with them. My friend and I would keep changing circles, which prevented us from making eye contact or conversing with anyone. It was after changing circles a couple of times that we entered a circle of English-speaking people. They were first-year university students from the UK. Here, my instincts told me to make eye-contact. I made eye-contact with one boy. I looked into his eyes. They were like two drops of coffee. He was tall, well-dressed and self-assured. He had a white shirt and black shorts on - a classic attire. As we were dancing, the circle eventually rotated to have both of us standing side by side. Instantly, I asked him his name. This was extremely unusual for my shy and timid nature. From there, our conversation was like a graph with a positive gradient. We talked for the rest of the time. That was the easiest conversation I have had with someone new. For the first time in a while, I felt butterflies in my stomach. There was something about the boy that I could not let be. That night, we exchanged our names on social media. I texted first, an oddly bold move for a girl like me. We kept in touch the next day and even bumped into each other at the beach - what were the odds, the very idea of fate finally came true in the fairy tale world I lived in. The night of the second day, we decided to meet. We both experienced a rough night before we were rewarded by a romantic walk. We went on a stroll with no destination. We indiscriminately held hands. It all happened so quickly and naturally, as if we knew each other for ages. We then sat at a bus stop. The nervousness sparked and I started rambling about how I do not usually do this with boys and how I usually keep to myself. I told him how overwhelmed I was and how I was not used to hanging out with a boy alone in this manner. I started babbling again. He then made me look into his macchiato eyes. The way it calmed me down was magical.

It was, then, time to leave. I was about to shed tears as I did not want the night to end. He embraced me tightly before we headed back. That night, as I entered the villa, my romantic bubble burst as I simultaneously burst into tears. I realised it was just a fling and that "the boy" was just like the "other boys". My heart, which felt complete for one night, now felt even smaller than before I met him. I felt even more empty and worthless.

For some reason, I was relying on a romantic partner for balance within my heart. I relied on their half to fit like a puzzle to mine to feel fulfilled. All I needed, though, was a glass of self-love to fill up my heart to feel the equilibrium.

Thought of the day: You can only rely on others when you have learnt the art of relying on yourself.

DAY 22/30

Social media includes the interactive technologies and digital channels that allow for the creation and sharing of information, ideas, interests and other forms of expression through virtual communities and networks.

I entered the social media world at quite a young age. Being able to connect with people in this parallel realm was mesmerising. It was the defenceless and insecure emotions that pulled me towards the use of online platforms. Every time I would feel sorrowful and unconfident, I would immediately resort to Instagram, the alpha of social media. As I would enter the chamber of the alpha, I would slowly get sucked in. I would take at least half an hour before coming back to the real world. The issue with this was that I would get sucked in without even realising it. Hours and hours would go by like time had no existence in this chamber. Slowly, as I walked down this chamber, my reality would get distorted and merged into the reality of the people I was viewing. For the mere minutes or hours, I would escape my life and be digitally living someone else's, it felt safe. It felt comfortable. It felt guarded. For the first couple of years of having social media, I had people around me to pull me out of the alpha's chamber. It was only when I started university, when I was alone, that I slowly lost control. At university, I relied on social media to deal with my problems. Entering the chamber, even when it said, "No entry", to deal with my real-world issues, caused me to start hearing voices and have no control over my actions.

It was a windy night at the end of November. The roughness of that day had chiselled my entire body by the time the sun had set. I, hence, resorted to my alpha for help, Instagram. That night, I started hearing voices. The voices had a high amplitude and low period. The heaviness of the sound trembled through my entire body. It started to take over the real me. It blinded me as it played its sounds in a hefty manner. It was that night that I started pushing people in the real world away from me, those who had lifejackets in their hands. The voices in my head had for the first time reached control over my entire body, rather than just my heart.

That night I succumbed to the voices. The voices in my head started working along with the alpha on a big project - destruction. It was only after being taken back by my parents and sleeping that I woke up to being my true self. My eyes could not believe the magnitude of the earthquake I had caused. 9.5! I could not believe the number of people that I had hurt that night. Next, I caused a tsunami. My entire house was filled with water leaking out of my eyes. Feeling regretful and frightened was an understatement. Regretful for not using the help I was offered and frightened because of the dual persona dormant within me. After this incident, I had become a sort of volcano that had eruptions in the pattern of a sine curve. Each curve was inevitable.

I had lost complete balance over my life. I wanted it to be a soundless graph, where there was not a single curve. Every night I slept afraid of a possible eruption the next day. Balance, where were you when I needed you the most?

Thought of the day: Social media is like a drug. Do not overdose!

DAY 23/30

Psychosis is when thoughts and emotions are so impaired that contact is lost with the external reality. Possible symptoms include delusions, hallucinations, agitations and talking incoherently. The person with the condition usually is not aware of his or her behaviour and can be of any age.

It all started a couple of weeks before university.

I was in a conversation with my parents and suddenly got one flashback of being lightly slapped by my mother for being naughty. This flashback entered my brain and caused it to create false memories. I, thus, became agitated at my parents. The memories that were created in my brain were like products produced by factory machines. Each memory would go from one machine to another to add detail by detail. I went to university in an irritable mood. This mood lingered in my cerebellum like a bouncing ball in a box. As months passed, the ball started growing in size. What it fed on, was non-existent memories about my parents. This small ball of agitation and delusion eventually turned bigger. Little did I know that this ball existed at the back of my brain feeding on the malfunctioning hippocampus. Despite all this happening and me attempting to push myself away from my parents, they remained the two pillars holding me back and protecting me from the outside world. At that time, I was blinded by carefully cooked up memories. The memories that my entire existence fed on was like unsavoury food. It used the worst ingredient - horrifying events that never took place.

How could it be possible? I was the diamond of my father's eye. He had already mined the diamond in me the night I was born. He knew his major existence on this planet was to help me notice the diamond within me. Being his first child and only girl, I meant more to him than anything else in the world. My mother was like a mother gorilla protecting her infant. Tough on the outside but protective and kind on the inside. There was no way she fit the terrifying descriptions my memories depicted. It was months later, when the bouncing ball had taken over all the positive memories I had of my parents.

One night, when all I was doing was pondering about the wrongdoings of my parents, I suddenly heard the sounds of firecrackers. I ran to my windowsill and sat there as the firecrackers grew in size, number and eventually covered the entire sky. Petrified, I called my parents - the first time in a month. I screamed for help. I was taken to therapy again. The same psychiatrist and the same psychologist. As I entered the room, I was still in denial about my flashbacks and recollections. It was when the psychiatrist started questioning certain instances that I slowly started snapping back into reality. The finger clicks were the therapy sessions slowly ushering me into reality again.

It was trust in my psychiatrist and my parents, despite my negative memories, that allowed the bouncing ball in my head, which caused me to feel out of equilibrium, to slowly decrease in size and eventually disappear to remind me of the feeling of balance.

Thought of the day: A change in mindset is the biggest cure.

DAY 24/30

Mindful eating - an approach to food that focuses an individual's sensual awareness of the food. It has little to do with calories, carbohydrates, fat or protein.

Due to always having a quick metabolism, gaining weight was never an issue for me. I could eat buckets and buckets of food while gaining only a few kilograms. But when I started treatment with the magical pills the mechanisms of my inner body started changing. The magical pills were needed to maintain balance in the systems of my brain. Like the magical beans from *Jack and the Beanstalk*, it grew a sort of beanstalk in my stomach. The beanstalk twirled and moved to change the inner workings of my body. This instilled the feelings of distress and demotivation. It was the first time that I had to be conscious and aware of the choices I made when it came to food. Although I always dreamed of this control, the change frightened me. As a child, I always moaned about not having control over the way I looked.

"Why don't you eat anything?" is what many asked. The truth was, I almost overate during every meal. My body just processed the food uniquely. I was always dejected by not putting on weight, despite the heavy meals I ate. My weight would never align with my height, the graph was always imbalanced. With the magical pills, I started off by not knowing how to use them. I did not know how to tame the beanstalk. I put on a lot of weight. Initially, it made me look healthy and allowed for a strong positive correlation between my weight and height. However, I needed to learn to control how to prevent further plunges. It was the maintenance of balance that I needed to master. Firstly, I started off by turning vegan. This helped me to conquer the cravings. I could only eat specific kinds of snacks. Since they were not that appetising, it prevented me from eating it. Turning vegan also prevented me from binge-eating at night. During the week though, if I had cravings, I would fulfil them by eating what I desired. In order to balance the cheat days, I made sure to work out at least twice a week. This made sure I would burn the unnecessary calories I gained.

Enslaving the beanstalk within me has taught me that balance is a lifestyle, not a one-time action.

Thought of the day: Being healthy is about incessantly fighting the unhealthiness, rather than suppressing it.

DAY 25/30

Failure is when there is a lack of success or inability to meet an expectation.

Growing up, the idea of failure was quite unfamiliar to me. I always worked hard to achieve the expectations and sometimes went beyond them. Failure was like a stranger that often came knocking on my door. Every time it knocked, I would ignore it and not open the door. During my school years, I never opened the door. But during my first year of university, when I was taken home to recover, Failure came knocking on my door again. This time, it knocked louder than usual, as if the door was about to break open. I had spent about four months at home recovering. We had to open the door. Standing there, tough and intimidating, was Failure. In its hand was a paper. The paper said that I had two options, either self-study the missed content at home, or repeat the year. I opted for the first choice. I tried self-studying. It worked for a month; however, gradually, I started losing motivation. Not being able to work in groups as per usual, or not having my teacher physically in class made me feel demotivated. Additionally, working on the tasks alone started bringing flashbacks. The words on the assignment slowly changed to become words of vivid incidents. We, thus, decided to repeat the year. We figured it was better for me as I would have the time to find myself and gain the usual university experience. Even though deep down I knew this was the right decision, the spirit of Failure had left its body and entered mine. Every day, my entire body would feel like it had surrendered to a higher power. A power from the underworld. I would wake up to find my entire body feeling bitter. I would always wake up saying, "I feel low." This bitter feeling caused by Failure would grow in size as the day prolonged. Inside me, Failure would go from spitting negative feelings to becoming a talking figure that took over the entirety of my body. It was one, loud and confident voice. The voice would continuously let me down. It worked like a drainage system, where every time it spoke, all the positivity, self-love and motivation would drain out quickly. All that was left was Failure, standing inside me boldly. I would cry for hours and hours trying to clog the drainage system but I just did not know how to do it. Every day, I relied on plumbers - family members and friends for help. However, the simple answer lied within the vast waters inside the drainage system. If the water would keep flowing forcefully, it would cause the drainage system to remain intact and balanced.

All I had to do was create a balanced routine of activities that kept me sane. The constant addition of mindful activities would be the addition of fresh water within the drainage system. This water would flow to create an equilibrium, slowly drowning Failure.

Thought of the day: Failure is just a perspective.

DAY 26/30

A solution is a means of solving a problem or dealing with a difficult situation.

During the four months of recovering at home, I was confronted with multiple issues. At the time, I had piles of problems and simply lacked the ability to solve them. What I understood by solving a problem was completely getting rid of the issue on the spot. What it actually meant was going through the problem and decreasing it eventually until it no longer exist. My problems had to do with my own wrongdoings. I had lost friends, had an increased emotion of guilt, lost purpose in life and completely detested myself. During the time of recovery, I was depressed. I could not see a single ray of light. All my issues mingled together to form a nest of depressive feelings in my gut. What I lacked was a means of unravelling the nest. I thought that there could be a way of getting hold of this nest and throwing it out. I thought that there existed a magic wand that could vanish the nest with a wave. I spent weeks and weeks weeping about how I missed family abroad. In my opinion at the time, their mere presence would have solved all my issues. I was wrong. All it would have done was place a blanket over the nest in my gut. When they would have left, they would have carried the blanket back with them. As the days passed, the nest started growing bigger. It started numbing the positivity in my body. I was unable to feel any happy emotions. Nothing brought me joy. All I knew how to do was sob. By the end of the four months, my house had been flooded with my tears. When I almost drowned in my tears, I started swimming and looking for answers. The answers were laid within the deep waters of my tears, within me. I realised that every time I would feel negative emotions, I would try and block the feelings. I would try and fight the nest inside me. What I should have done, though, was let the nest poke and hurt my body as I stroked and petted it. I should have undergone the emotions and acknowledged what the nest had to say. This would have then allowed me to not extract the positivity and happiness within me.

Slowly slowly as I learnt how to deal with my feelings instead of fighting to get rid of them, I learnt the art of balancing the positive and negative sides of me. I was able to get rid of the nest as it had nothing to feed on. Hours and hours of crying had now changed to minutes of small breakdowns, where the nest would show up, but would leave as it did not get the attention it sought for - someone willing to fight it.

Thought of the day: Going through your emotions, instead of barring them is the best solution.

DAY 27/30

A support system is the network of people who provide an individual with practical or emotional support.

My support system was quite unclear to me until I spent four months isolated from the outside world. I would spend days and days crying copiously. Pools of tears that would dry and slowly disappear under the sun. It felt like I had a black gas slithered in my chest. It was pumped out of my rotten heart and suffocated me. Under the gas was a black nest. A nest, as mentioned before, that changed in size and blocked the positivity in me as it grew. The nest was negativity scribbled into one structure. Under the nest was an invisible sphere. A sphere that let out waves of guilt. It travelled as fast as light and felt like tickles running down the entirety of my body. It felt as though my body was made up of these very organs controlled by an overarching, inner voice and that the rest of my body had become paralysed. Everyday, I would wonder where those that cared about me went. I wondered why family abroad or friends at university would not be there physically to help me undergo the pain.

When I entered one of my therapy sessions with drooping and watery eyes I explained my feelings with imagery. During the session, I was told to close my eyes. I was told to imagine all my loved ones, my support system, as little people. I had to imagine them as small people within my body, carrying the three imaginary and burning organs out of my body. I had to imagine them present within me, sewing the cracks and scratches of my wounded heart. I had to visualise them growing roots from my heart. Roots that grew down my body and went through my feet to eventually go beneath the ground. Roots that kept me grounded enough to deal with the criticising and condemning inner voice. When I opened my eyes, the chaos inside my body had decreased. The war between the imaginary and existing organs had slowly settled. I came to the revelation that heaven and hell are the needlecrafts of our own visualisations. What felt like hell, slowly turned into specks of heavenly emotions as I changed my thoughts and mental images.

I realised that one's support system does not need to be physically present to help maintain balance within one's life. Their mere presence in the heart and thoughts is more than enough. Their love needs to be strong enough so that the strings that attach people's hearts are not cut down by negative thoughts and visualisations.

Thought of the day: One only insists to see when there is a lack of belief.

DAY 28/30

Self-reflection is the ability to witness and evaluate our own cognitive, emotional and behavioural processes.

It was during the four months of hibernation that I started contemplating the events that had taken place during the outbursts. I started looking at them as one would look at reflections of the sky onto lakes or ponds. At first, the details were a blur, but as I examined them more deeply, I slowly started recollecting the details. The first outburst, the biggest bomb let off, was what I dissected first. I remember how I was sucked into my phone and how my phone had complete control over what I was doing. I remember feeling as though all the inner workings and threads connecting the systems of my brain had let loose and that my brain had completely shut down. My brain was replaced by the workings of my phone. These memories put together allowed me to understand my emotions of guilt as it assured me that my wrongdoings were unintentional. It was a mishap in my brain that led me to take action with everything that was before me and anything that was the quickest to reach. At the time, wrong and right were mingled into one. Then there was the relapse. Here, the threads of my brain slowly unravelled again and gave in to my phone. I spent three days with my brain having no connection with the rest of my body parts. Additionally, the three nights were sleepless, hence there was no ability for my brain to revamp and connect the threads again. Here again, understanding that I was unconscious and possessed by my phone, allowed me to become one with the rippling effects of guilt in my gut. Slowly, as I understood every scenario that took place, calls, text messages and posts, I realised that I could never explain why I did what I did. It was as though a stronger power over me simply became deranged and started to demolish everything it came in contact with. It broke all the fences of protection - which were those that attempted to help - and harmed everything inside - which was everything that had nothing to do with me. This left nothing but my possessed self in the middle of destruction. When I was lonely again and had no means of contact, the evil spirit left my body and got sucked into my phone again. I was able to acknowledge the guilty sphere within me by solving my outbursts like a word problem and reflecting on the answers.

As I acknowledged it, it grew smaller in size, letting out less powerful waves through my body. This enabled me to feel more balanced as I attempted to listen to what the negative emotions within me had to say. It brought me to equilibrium as my guilt was not fought against, and was just heard, recognised and reflected upon.

Thought of the day: There exists bridges of self-observation on the road to growth.

DAY 29/30

Gratitude: It is the state of self-contentment and acceptance of life as it flows. It is a feeling of appreciation.

It was during the recuperation stage of my condition that I understood the vitality of gratitude. Gratitude was like a gas that I breathed in and out. A gas that had been invisible my entire life, but slowly started becoming visible to me as the days passed. Gratitude worked like a key that opened a door behind which all the answers to my pain lied. The reasons as to why I felt depressed could be found with the feelings of thankfulness.

It was a bright sunny day in the middle of the winter, when my father woke me up eagerly. He pulled my blankets off me and excitedly told me to follow him. In a grumpy mood, I followed his footsteps to the balcony.

"Look!" he said.

"What? There is nothing new. All I see is the sky, clouds and trees," I replied.

"Don't you see it? The sky is bright blue, the clouds are shining in white and the trees have started growing leaves again."

"But isn't that what we see every day?"

"That is what you *think* you see every day. How many times do you come outside on the balcony to simply appreciate nature and thank the Universe for the little changes it makes? Yesterday, I stood here like we are standing today and noticed the weather and surroundings. It was cold, grey and everything was dull. This morning, however, was the first time we received a sunlit morning in weeks," he said patiently.

This stuck with me. I realised how I always focused on what my life lacked, rather than thanking the Universe for the little positive changes it made. From that day on, I decided to start bayleaf therapy, one of the many therapies to show gratitude. I did this every day for months. Slowly, I started noticing how the miniscule and unnoticed changes in my life turned into bigger, more helpful and impactful changes. I started to see the particles of the gratitude gas flow in and out of my body, the particles that flowed out was my gratitude let out to the Universe and what flowed in was what the Universe did to help me. The way in which gratitude works is exactly like oxygen. 16.4 percent of oxygen is exhaled, while 21 percent is inhaled. This shows that the amount of gratitude performed and felt will lead to larger results from the Universe. Understanding this concept allowed me to pinpoint every reason as to why I felt low. I would question why I was not grateful for something and immediately figure out the root cause, making me feel better. Instead of acting upon my low feelings, I simply went through them by applying the ideology of gratitude.

Through experiencing how gratitude worked, I realised that it was what gave balance the energy to exist. It was as though the inhaling of the gas of gratitude allowed balance to grow from within. Without gratitude, there would be no balance.

Thought of the day: Nurturing gratitude, with the ingredients of belief and spiritual conviction, brings magic to your doorstep.

DAY 30/30

Balance - a situation in which different elements are equal or in correct proportions. It is the even distribution of weight enabling someone or something to remain upright and steady.

Imagine sitting on a seesaw on one end so that the seesaw is tipping towards your side. On your back is a bag full of elements of aid that are needed to master the art of balance. What are you to do? You are to slowly remove the elements from the bag and place them on the other side of the seesaw so that the seesaw slowly has equal weights on either side, gaining equilibrium. Carrying the elements from one side to another is easy; however, keeping them from falling off is the challenge. Achieving balance is one thing, but maintaining it is another.

Maintaining balance is where the upgrade in life lies. In order to maintain balance, you would have to glue the elements of aid onto the seesaw. This would prevent them from falling. What must this glue be composed of? A mixture of perseverance, optimism and piety.

Perseverance - persistently including a lifestyle that brings your life into equilibrium, despite the difficulty or delay it causes in bringing success.

Optimism - hopefulness and confidence about the future, even when there are downfalls and periods of severe ruination.

Piety - loyalty to the idea of achieving balance; treating balance like a religion and the actions to achieving it as a form of worship.

The elements of aid in the bag are collected as we walk our paths on Earth. Hence, all elements are not always present; one has to go through certain experiences to have them. As time passes, our weights do not remain constant. This causes the seesaw to slightly tip towards one side every time there is a small increase or decrease in mass. Sometimes, elements of aid are not present in the backpack. What must one do in a situation like this? This is where faith comes in. Faith in the religion of balance, knowing it exists even if it cannot be seen or heard, allows the seesaw to move that small centimetre back to regain equilibrium. An important aspect to be considered here is to understand that everyone sits on a different seesaw and has different elements of aid on their backs. Additionally, everyone follows the religion of balance with a different level of faith. Therefore, comparing one's life to another based on the achievement of balance is pointless. Comparing, nevertheless, the consequences of balance and what changes it brings to one's life is comparable. A balanced seesaw's impact on people's daily lives is thoroughly noticeable and distinguishable. Another aspect that is essential to understand about balance is that it is a unique type of religion. One would think there are certain norms or rules that are followed by the majority of the disciples. The truth is, you are simply given an empty Bible, on which you are to write your own rules that bring balance to your life. There is no God to pray to. God resides within us, as well as in our surroundings or the Universe.

Now, the choice is yours. Are you willing to sit on the seesaw of balance and start your never ending journey?

Thought of the day: Being religious means being consistent.

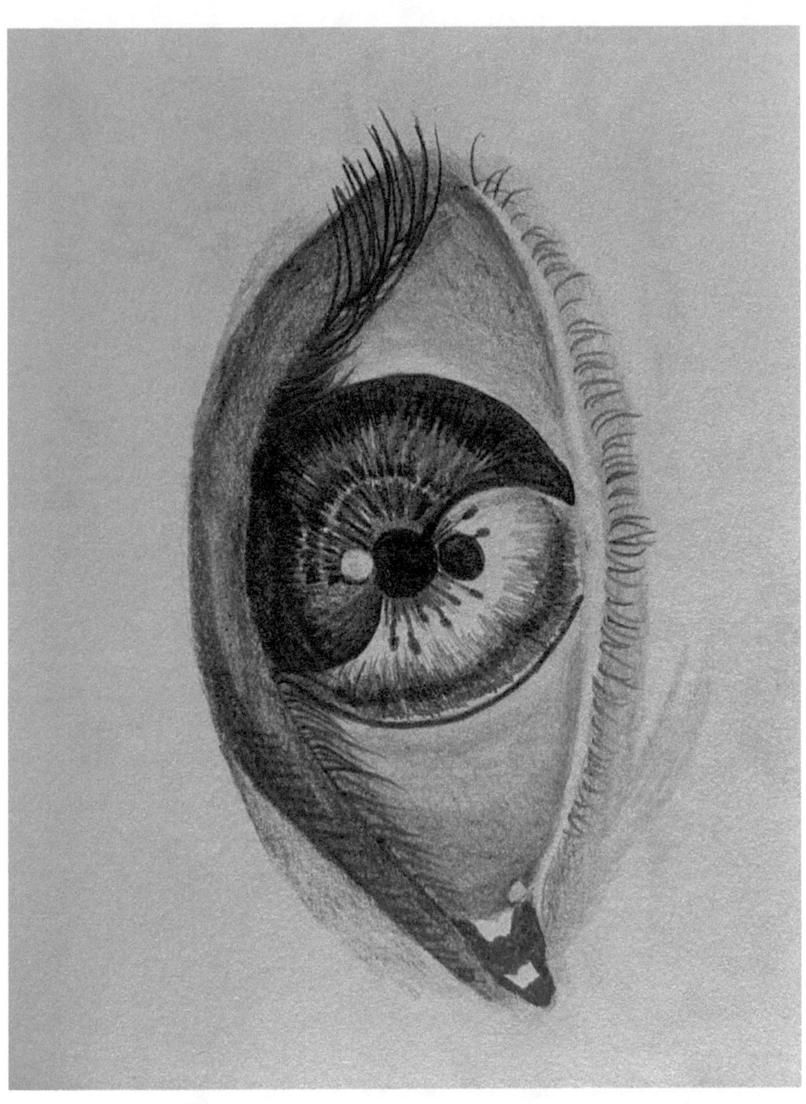

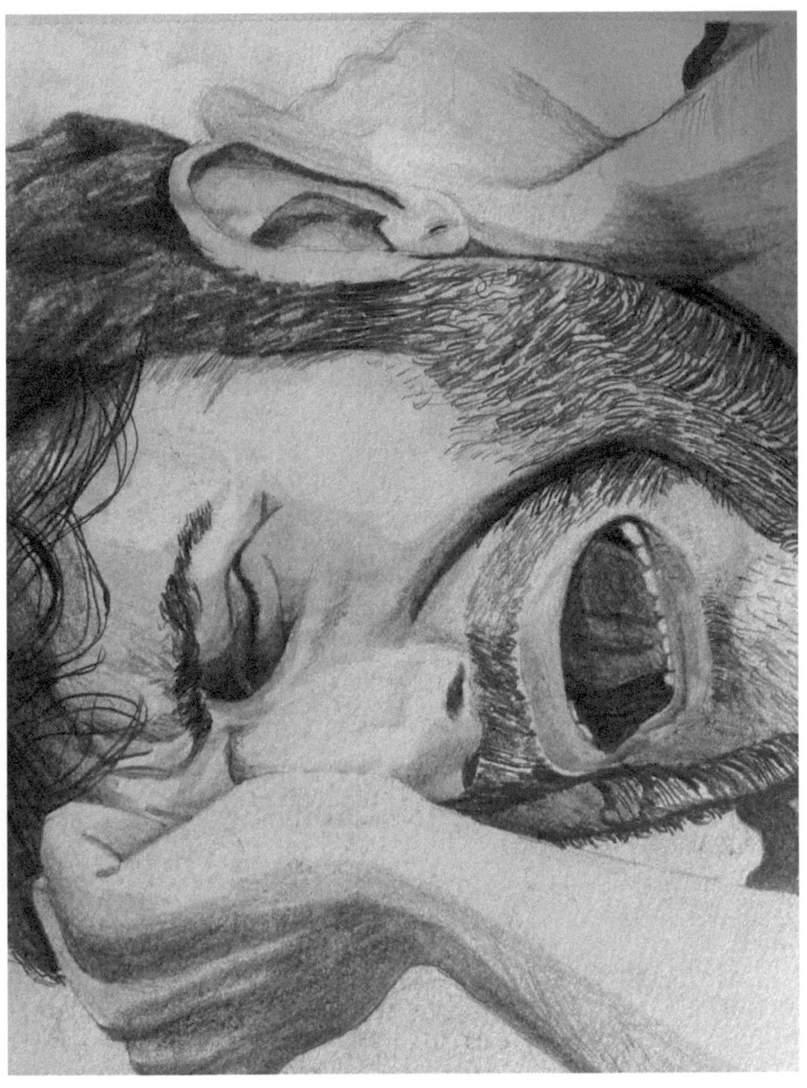

PART II

THE CROWN AND TWO FLUKES OF AN ANCHOR

Standing there, five floors above the ground, I stood with a fixed mindset. My eyes followed the heavy clouds above as they slowly made way from one side of the sky to another. I could feel the heaviness of the clouds in my gut. My hands, glued to the railings behind me, dripped with sweat as I clasped tighter and tighter. I slowly turned my head downwards to have the view of Mumbai's mid-afternoon disorderly traffic. I leaned forward and slowly released my hands. Down I flew, with my eyes zipped shut. I was a dove finally achieving its ultimate freedom. I accelerated towards the ground. I was about to land flat on my body when I suddenly felt softness. I unzipped my eyes to find myself under my blanket, tucked in safely like a butterfly in its cocoon. I untucked myself and sat up straight. I felt the birds of dizziness above my head and could not stay straight. As I slowly stood up and made my way out of my bed, I felt like an atom that lacked its nucleus and protons and only consisting of orbiting electrons. As I tried walking, it felt as though the electrons started orbiting faster. I felt as though I was tipping towards one side. Unbalanced. Slowly, I started feeling tears drop down my cheeks like water drips down leaves when it rains. As I made my way out of my room, I created puddles of water that left a trail behind me. The puddles started becoming bigger the further I walked. By this time, the electrons were moving at a speed faster than light. The uneasiness that it caused inside me was uncontrollable.

"No one understands the pain. The guilt. No one feels what I feel."

These were the only words that came out of my mouth. These words made it a struggle for those around me to truly understand what I was feeling. I resorted to actions. I started throwing pillows and moving furniture. I had almost hit rock bottom. My balance was so out of place that I was about to tip over, when suddenly I remembered that my sinking boat had an anchor. An anchor with a crown and two flukes - my older brother and twin sisters. Shaking, I grabbed my phone and called my older brother immediately. He was my guide, advisor and protector. With his calmness and compassion, he was able to slow down the electrons around me. Then, I called my twin sisters. One of them acted like the missing nucleus, while the other acted like the proton. Their patience, logic and ability to listen slowed down the electrons even more. They both worked together as a team, as if they re-joined to become one embryo, to bring me to my senses. All three of my cousins enabled me to regain my equilibrium. They ensured that my vessel did not descend. They saved me.

Moral of the story: Every boat has an anchor, but using the anchor is a choice that you have to make.

SUPERWOMEN

It was the night I had returned home from university. As I entered my house, everything was still blurry. I could not recognize the people around me. Heaviness diffused down my body from my head to my feet, eventually making me unable to walk properly. I felt stuck. Heaviness kept moving up and down inside my body. Suddenly, I started shivering. Faster and faster as I felt the nerves in my brain sending random signals. Unable to understand where I had entered and recognise the people at home I started screaming for help. Scared, I ran into the kitchen and slammed a glass onto the floor. As the glass shattered around me, I fell onto the floor and started wailing. I was crying for help. Immediately, I felt a soft touch. It felt as though a feather had landed on my shoulder. The mere touch lessened my crying and slowed down my shivering. I looked up. It was a young and sweet-looking girl who had reached for my shoulders. She looked into my eyes and made a connection with my soul.

"Are you hungry?" she asked me. Despite not recognising her, my soul simply dragged my body to follow her. I sat on a chair beside the dining table with her. The girl sat there with me and started telling me stories about her endeavours of working as a nurse in Nepal, as well as stories about how she met her husband. There was something about the way her eyes twinkled that was very comforting. By the time her story had ended, I looked down at my plate and the food had vanished. I was confused as to how easily the food moved down my oesophagus. Then, the girl held me with her warm hands and took me to my room. As I was still slightly shivering, she started rubbing my back. It was like she was transferring love from her body to mine. Slowly, I started regaining consciousness and the connection with the real-world. Everything was not blurry anymore. I realised where I was and recognised everyone around me. I recognised the young girl in front of me. She was the house help. The love with which she did everything allowed my brain to regain balance and start functioning properly. I tightly embraced her as an act of appreciation.

Sadly, I had to bid adieu to this help as she had brighter plans for her future as a nurse. She was replaced by another young girl. On her first day, as she entered the house she could hear me weeping. I, again, could not see anything clearly. Everything around me was spinning. As everything turned faster, tears started rolling down my cheeks. Morning after morning, the new help would enter the house to loud cries, until one day she said something. She quietly dragged me to the kitchen and began talking. She told me about her experiences of running away and getting married at the age of eighteen; going to study in Japan; leaving her studies to move places for her husband's work; losing friends. An invisible force formed between us as she described her hardships. It was empathy. It reset the neurons in my brain and calmed me down. Knowing that there was someone that understood my pain, guilt and melancholy rewired my system to slowly gain equilibrium.

Moral of the story: Help will reach you in various forms. Judging its origin will cause it to slip through your fingers.

HEART OF A RUBY

It was the first day of school. One of the classes that I had was French. As I walked down the corridor without knowing what to expect from my teacher, I felt the nervousness and anxiety in the dripping sweat of my palms. I entered the room. Unlike all the other rooms I felt a gush of warm air land on my face and surround my body like a cosy blanket would on a cold winter night. It smelled like jasmine flower, which is symbolic of love, purity and feminine powers. This scent energised me. It felt as though a charger got plugged into me, the air being the charger and my body the socket. It energised me positively. As I sat down on the desk, I noticed how I had stopped sweating. How was this possible? No contact with anyone and I had already started feeling better. There was magic in the aura. Suddenly I heard footsteps. As the steps got closer, my heart started pounding faster, finding a way to escape my body. Finally, she entered, a mid-aged woman, walking with a posture that announced dignity and respect. Her hair was done exquisitely, braided with detail and then tied up in a bun. Furthermore, her outfit perfectly matched her complexion. She looked me in the eye. Instead of feeling intimidated, I felt comforted. The classroom had immediately started feeling less conventional and more homely.

"We've got a new student!"

She yelled excitedly with a beaming smile. I had not seen anyone this excited about me in ages. As we started with some exercises, she immediately pointed out, "Why are you so afraid of making mistakes?" My jaw dropped as I was taken aback. It was the first time in my entire existence that someone understood my deepest fears. As those words came out of her mouth, a bond was formed. An unbreakable connection.

Fast forward to when I was in university. It was the first night that I started feeling discomforted and uneasy, the night my symptoms had started showing up. Immediately, I called my teacher. She was the first person that came to mind. Perhaps it was her warmth and wisdom that I longed for. As she lived far from me, the next day, I was invited to her daughter's house for dinner. Her daughter, just like her, had a heart of a ruby. She was pure, noble and mellow. She made me a warm cup of hot chocolate after our meal. It was like a potion filled with love that gave me the power to carry on my fight against my imbalances. My teacher, who could not be there with me, ensured I was safe and sound with her daughter. From that day onwards, she kept checking on me. The mere existence of me in her thoughts and prayers kept me going. It was as though she was sending me strength telepathically. Our bond was resurrected every time we talked. Our bond gave me the energy to regain equilibrium. Our bond gave me balance.

Moral of the story: It is during your darkest times that the strongest bonds unveil.

MOTHERLY SAVIOUR

Weeks and weeks had passed since I had been at home recovering from my first outburst. It was a rollercoaster ride; some days I felt low, while some other days felt more positive. It was a sunny morning, when I woke up feeling slightly uncomfortable. The weather was deceptive as it did not portray the feelings I felt on the inside. As I got out of bed, I felt the tears slowly racing down my cheeks. One by one, they increased in speed as they escaped my tear ducts. As I left my room, I felt the negative emotions getting stronger. Eventually, these feelings pulled me to the dark, delusional space. I was no longer the eighteen-year-old girl my parents knew. I had completely lost myself again. My parents struggled to talk to me and bring me back to reality. Hence they called over a family friend. She rushed to our house immediately. She sat by me and comforted me. There was something about her aura. Her words were a blur to me, but her warmth touched me, surpassing the guarded shield that had formed when I entered the black space. Slowly, after hours of conversation, she brought me back to reality. My body was no longer numb. Before the family friend left, she glanced into my eyes. It was like she was trying to unravel the fiery feelings within me.

She frowned and said, "Do you want me to stay over and sleep with you tonight? Are you sure you are alright?"

The masked smile on my face was not enough to fool her. As much as I did not want to be a burden to her, I knew I needed her. It was on this day that I started believing in fairy tales. She was my fairy godmother. I felt a deep connection to her despite having no genes in common.

"Yes, please," I mumbled to her. That night, she slept with me. We started by watching a movie together. Then, I fell asleep. About an hour later, I started shivering and shaking. I could not control the movements of my body. My body had succumbed to extreme restlessness. Next to me, my motherly saviour stroked my head. She started pressing my feet and massaging my arms to calm me down, and to re-join the broken connections of my brain. It did not work. She felt helpless. She knew she could only resort to one solution. She started meditating and praying for me. She stroked my head simultaneously. She sacrificed her sleep that night just to put me to sleep. The next morning, her eyes were baggy, swollen and surrounded by dark circles. I immediately gave her a tight hug before she left. Ever since that day she was a significant part of my recovery. She ensured that I worked out, ate right and had some fun in my monotonous life. She was a friend, a mother and a pillar. She made sure I did not waver from my equilibrium. She was one of the reasons I could continue my journey to reach the balance I had lost.

Moral of the story: People enter your lives at the right time and for the right reasons. Some teach you lessons, while others help you through it.

SPIRITUAL AWAKENING

After a month of having slowly pieced my life back together, where I no longer had daily outbursts, did not spend the whole day in bed, worked out and occasionally started going out with my family, destiny led me to a life-changing encounter. My parents always tried to convince me to incorporate meditation into my routine. For some reason, however, I could not concentrate and it never seemed to help me. One day, my mom decided to take me to someone who held guided meditations. As I entered this lady's house, a peculiar feeling of familiarity gushed through my body. As I climbed up the stairs to her meditation room, the feeling got stronger. There, she was. As I looked her in the eyes for the first time, there was a sense of familiarity; a sense of having met her before. Before we commenced with meditation, the lady wanted to know a little about me and what brought me to her. I thought I would answer with a short sentence and we would move onto meditating; however, that question led to an hour of conversing. The discussion was so smooth and easy. We had so much in common with our experiences. She gave me insightful information from her personal experience and readings. She explained to me how everything in our lives happens for a reason. How we are doomed to suffer from karmas we accumulated either from our past lives or current ones. She mentioned how we were all souls in bodies trying to reach ultimate peace, which in turn is reaching ultimate purity, a state where you have no karmas. From then on, it all started making sense to me. "Why did I have to suffer? What did I do to deserve this?" The questions were slowly answered.

The lady explained the purpose of meditation. She told me how it helps attaining inner peace by finding answers from within. That day, we did not get time to meditate, but I was already open to incorporating it into my life. As I left the room, my eyes were drawn to two big portraits. Instantly I felt an electrifying feeling. A feeling of hope. I felt a sort of attachment to the two people in the photographs. I asked the lady who they were.

"Sri Aurobindo and The Mother," she said. Immediately, I felt a quick shiver. I realised my sole purpose of living. I suddenly had a deep, longing desire to help those in need. No matter what career path I would take, I knew this was something I had to incorporate. This desire attached to my body like how a missing piece would attach to complete a puzzle. I realised that to start feeling whole again, this is what I needed to do.

The next few times I went to the lady's house, I meditated. It was on my third meditation session, that something miraculous happened. I saw The Mother placing her hand on my head to bless me. I then saw Sri Aurobindo on top of a rapid river trying to grab a bowl of holy water to bless me with. As I opened my eyes, I realised that guardian angels do exist. I had found mine. That is when I knew that I had to visit Auroville in Pondicherry to gain a deeper connection with Sri Aurobindo and the Mother. After a few weeks of meditating with the lady and opening the layers of my higher self, I finally took a trip to India, where I spent two days in Auroville. I took part in group meditations, spent time in The Mother's room and took blessings from the Samadhi, where Sri Aurobindo and The Mother were buried. After that trip, I felt as though I had no reason to worry anymore. Any problem that I had, I asked Sri Aurobindo and The Mother for help. There was no looking back from then on. I continued meditating to allow myself to walk on my spiritual journey ahead, where I tried to slowly unravel the true reasons for my being. As I walked down this path, I found a way to control my outbursts and live a more fulfilling lifestyle. A lifestyle with more mental balance.

Moral of the story: Traumatic experiences can be one of the keys to evolve. Either you learn from them and progress, or you continue to suffer.

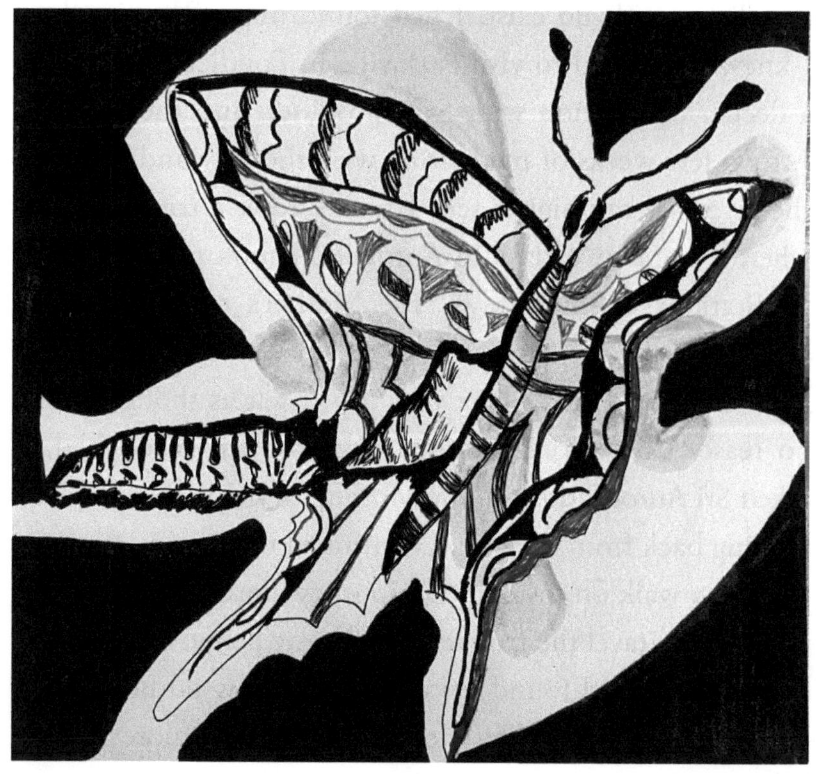

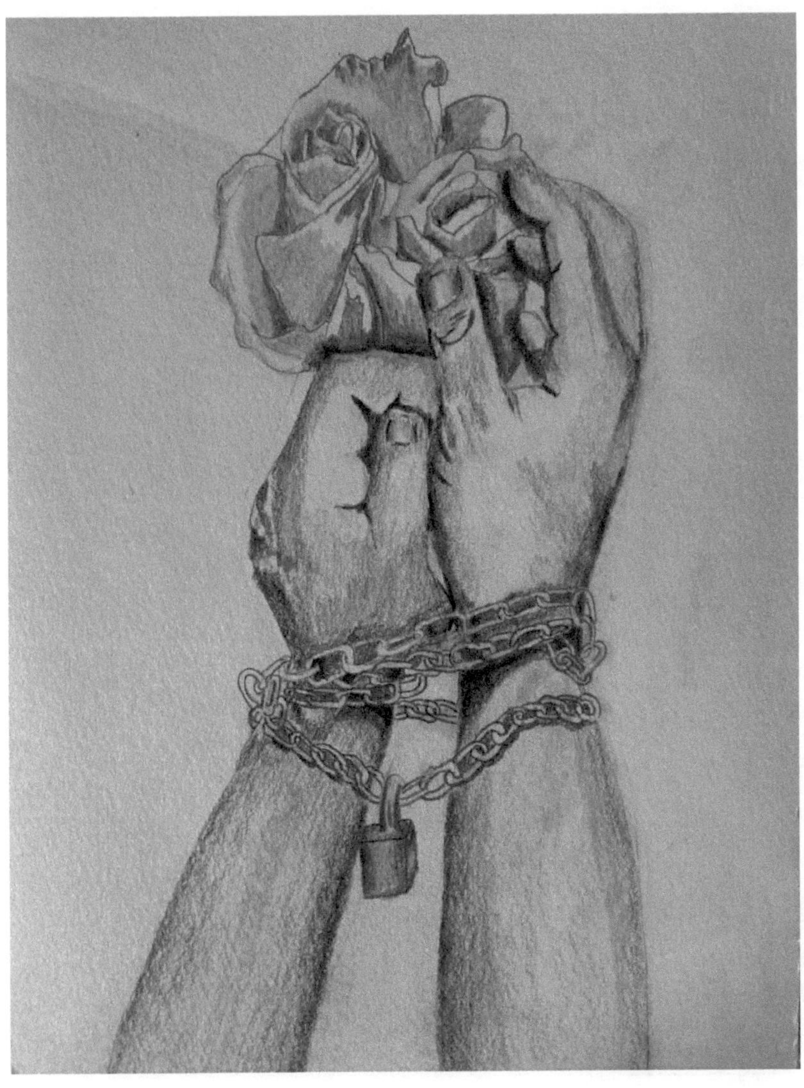

PART III

THE RISING PHOENIX

Maintaining a consistent, healthy lifestyle is as difficult as completely getting rid of a mental illness. For many disorders, the aftermath is extremely tough to fight. Psychosis came to me like a tsunami. The wave hit my body and destroyed every part from within. Hence, after it had left, my body was benumbed. My entire inner being had been killed; all that was left was the mere physical body I had. This caused a sort of mourning after my recovery. Yes, I no longer had outbursts and no longer experienced the symptoms of my illness, but I started experiencing depression. This is common for many as during the moments of self-reflection one realises that they are no longer the same person they were. All emotions were ripped out of me and there was no hope for the future. I mourned for the person I was before my disorder. Thus, instead of my mental health being disrupted by daily outbursts, it was disrupted by crying and constant sadness. Many nights, I would just walk out to my balcony and stare down. I would then close my eyes and imagine what it was like to let loose and free myself from my body. When my emotions would overcome my thoughts in this manner, I would ask for help. Deep down, under all the layers of negativity, there was a girl screaming for help. Vocalising my feelings was significant in my recovery. With the guidance of others, I was more motivated. Instead of working out three times a week, I tried to do it every day. Instead of sitting home and being unproductive, I decided to join an online course on fashion. I also started going out more often. I went shopping, watched movies and occasionally ate out too. On days that I felt low, instead of sulking and ruining my day, I called up friends or family members and vented it out. As days passed, I was able to slowly climb out of my depressed phases. I could feel the fire below my feet slowly disappearing as my wings started growing bigger.

I could sense rebirth. The person that died by psychosis, was now slowly being reborn. This rebirth was facilitated by trust, positivity, persistence and most importantly, hope.

Now, here I am, sitting on the very same balcony. Instead of ending the chance I have to make a difference, I am sitting here and appreciating the second shot I have at living life. Instead of being saddened by my past, I am full of acceptance and understanding of the hardships I went through, to learn and grow. I am grateful for my experiences as I am now wiser and stronger than before. Reflection: Everyone is lucky that God gave them a life. I was lucky to be given two.

NOW WHAT?

Who would have thought that a life-changing journey could have positive effects? It is all about perspective - choosing to look at the brighter side. Here I am, the same young girl who still has big dreams. Here I am, a young girl who is now way beyond her year, a girl who is wiser and stronger. Here I am, living in the same old world, but with a new pair of eyes. Someone wise once told me: "In order to love who you are, you cannot hate the experiences that shaped you."

The last step to complete recovery was looking back and replaying the bitter memories with a smile. Yes, I was broken, in pain and in loss. However, the past cannot be undone. It was fate. What is in our hands, though, is how we choose to let the past affect our present and future. As someone who has gone through immense difficulties, I know that it is easier said than done; but I also know that it is possible. I am here, not carrying my past as baggage, but as a ladder that lifts me higher. Now, the empty career and travel goals in my head have been overloaded with ideas.

Travel Bucket List:

- [ ] Safaris in South Africa/Botswana
- [ ] Ski trip with family
- [ ] Skydiving in South Africa
- [ ] Northern Lights in Iceland
- [ ] Dead Sea in Israel
- [ ] Scuba diving
- [ ] Cherry Blossoms in Japan
- [ ] Trekking in Leh Ladakh
- [ ] Road trip to Scandinavia
- [ ] Tomatina festival in Spain
- [ ] Colour run
- [ ] Tomorrowland
- [ ] Witness a flash mob

Career Bucket List:

- [ ] Bachelor's degree
- [ ] Master's degree
- [ ] Intern with a luxury fashion house
- [ ] Create a brand to help make fashion more sustainable.
- [ ] Write a book
- [ ] Start a YouTube channel

Above includes all my ideas for now. It is only a temporary bucket list and can change over time.

Balance has not only made me healthy, but it has also given me reason. It has given me purpose. Every day, instead of dreading the sunlight that awakens me, I appreciate how its rays sparkle and bless me every morning.

Reflection: Recovery is not only about being healthier, but it is also about reflection. It is about shifting your mindset to a meta-perspective.

ABOUT THE AUTHOR

Aayushi Mehta is a young Indian girl who was born and brought up in a small town called Antwerp, in Belgium. She is currently studying Fashion in Amsterdam. Growing up in a closely knit Indian community, she has been able to form deep connections with her root culture. Aayushi always had an eye for creativity and is a talented artist. Other hobbies include dancing, travelling and playing tennis.

SUMMARY

On a late night in November, I saw my whole life flash before me. Everything that I worked towards was taken away in a split second. I lost my first year at university, my friends and most importantly, myself. The cause was Psychosis. You must be thinking, what exactly is that? That is one of the reasons for the existence of this book.

Sure, you can google the illness and learn the symptoms, but this book elucidated the true experience of a young girl who underwent these symptoms. Dealing with mental health and eventually suffering from psychosis is broken down into experiences and life lessons. This book destigmatises mental health by depicting the journey of rediscovering myself and the search for the soul beneath my flesh. When an individual soul is silently trying to fit into the normalcy of the external world's realities, they can encounter hurdles in many different forms. But for those in loss of hope, self-love and ambition, this book is the cure.

Printed by Libri Plureos GmbH in Hamburg, Germany